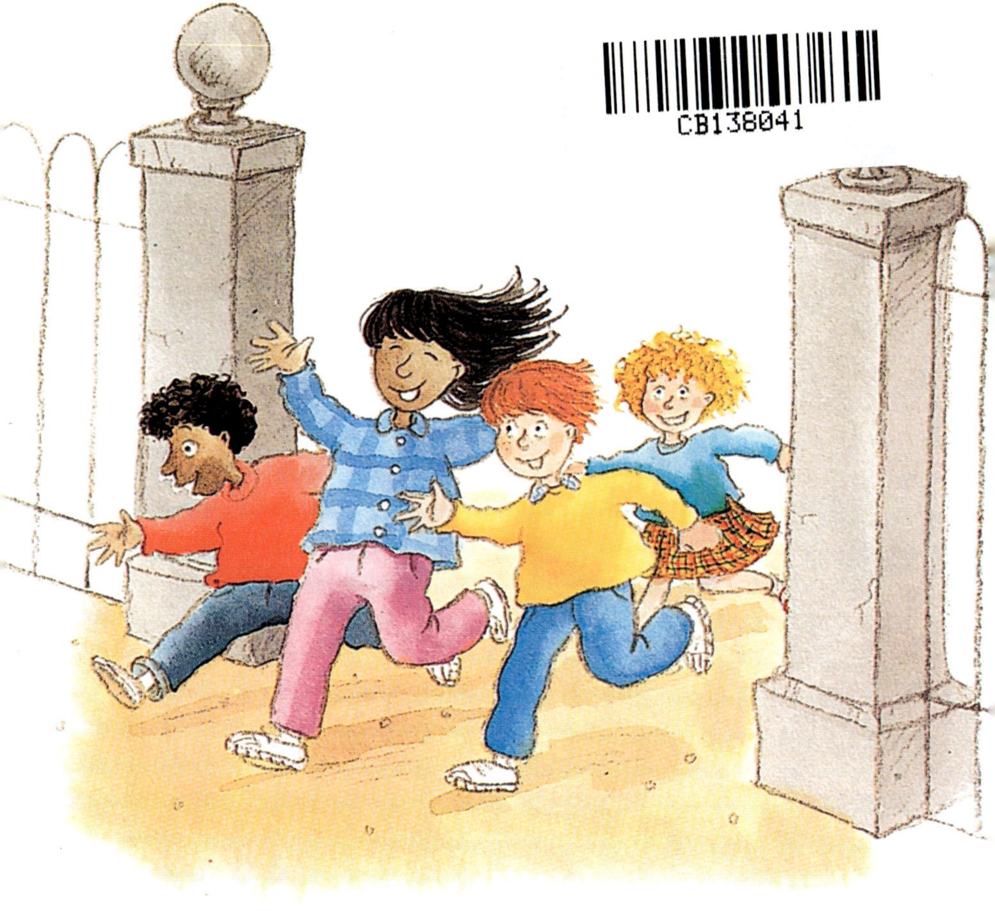

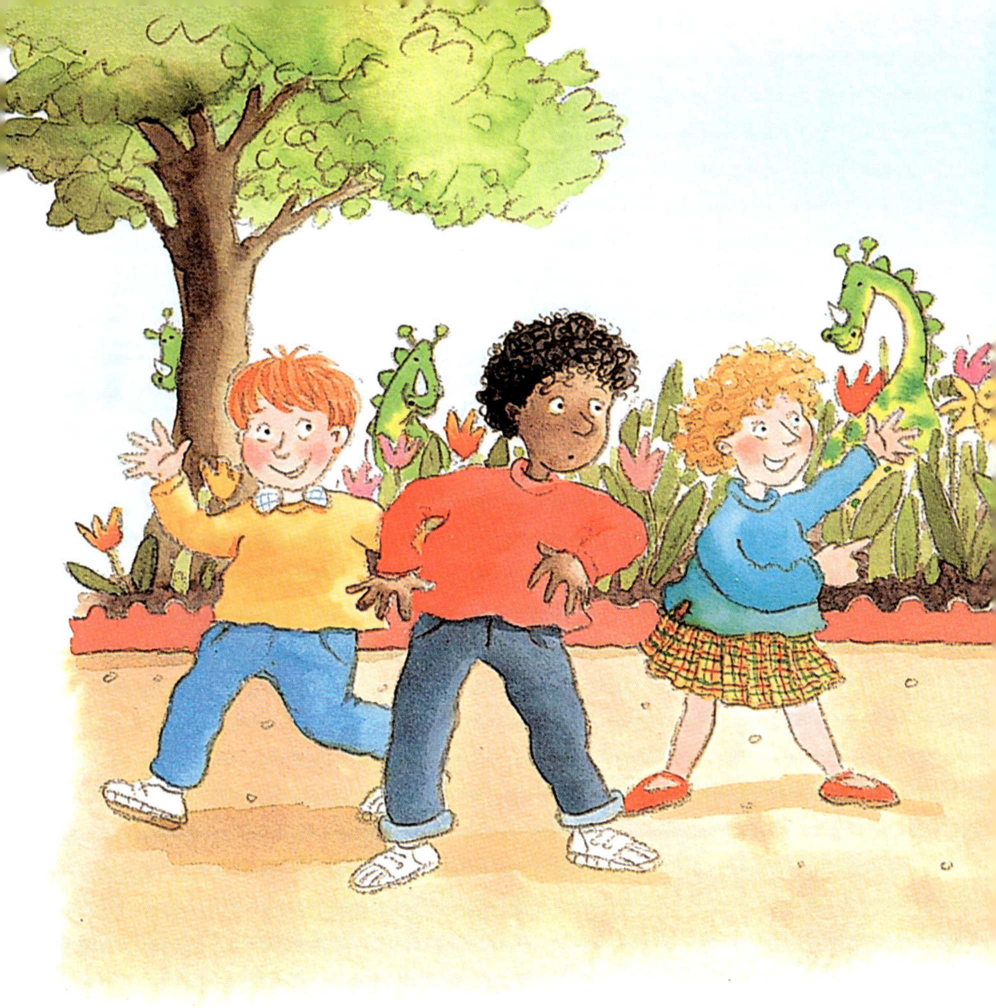

What can we do today?

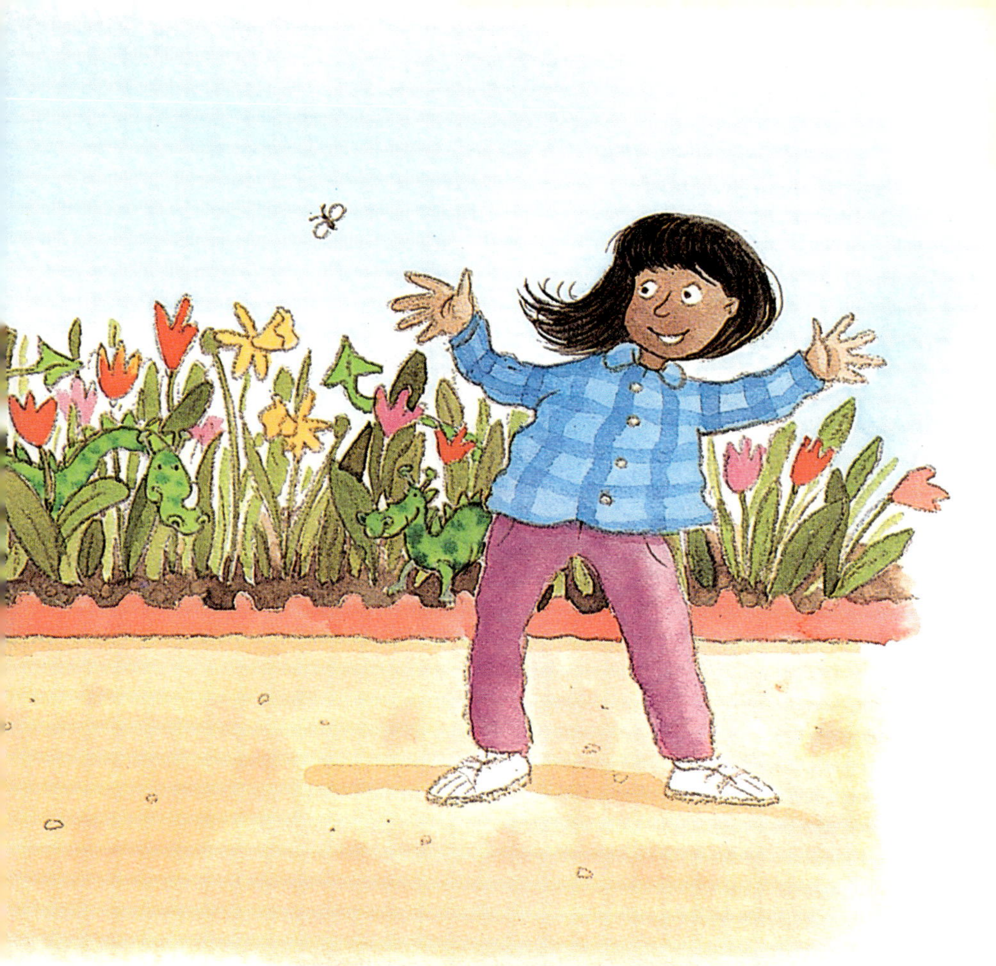

Look for dragons!

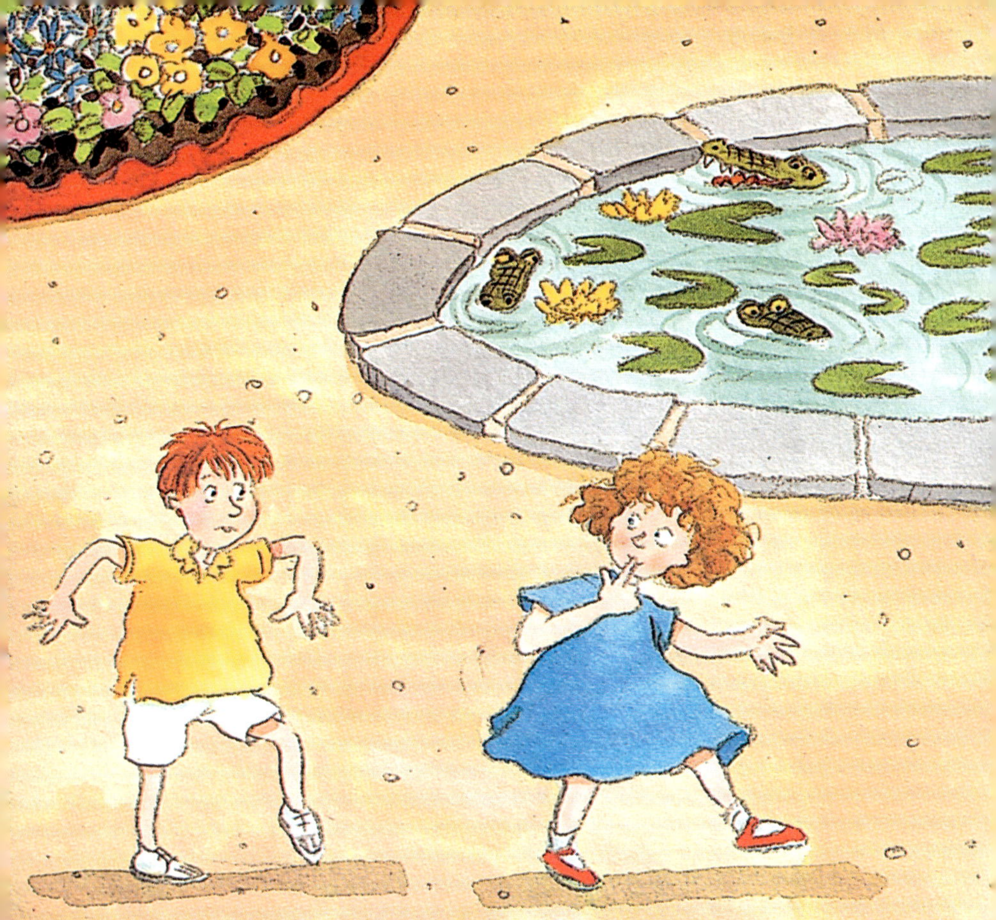

What can we do today?

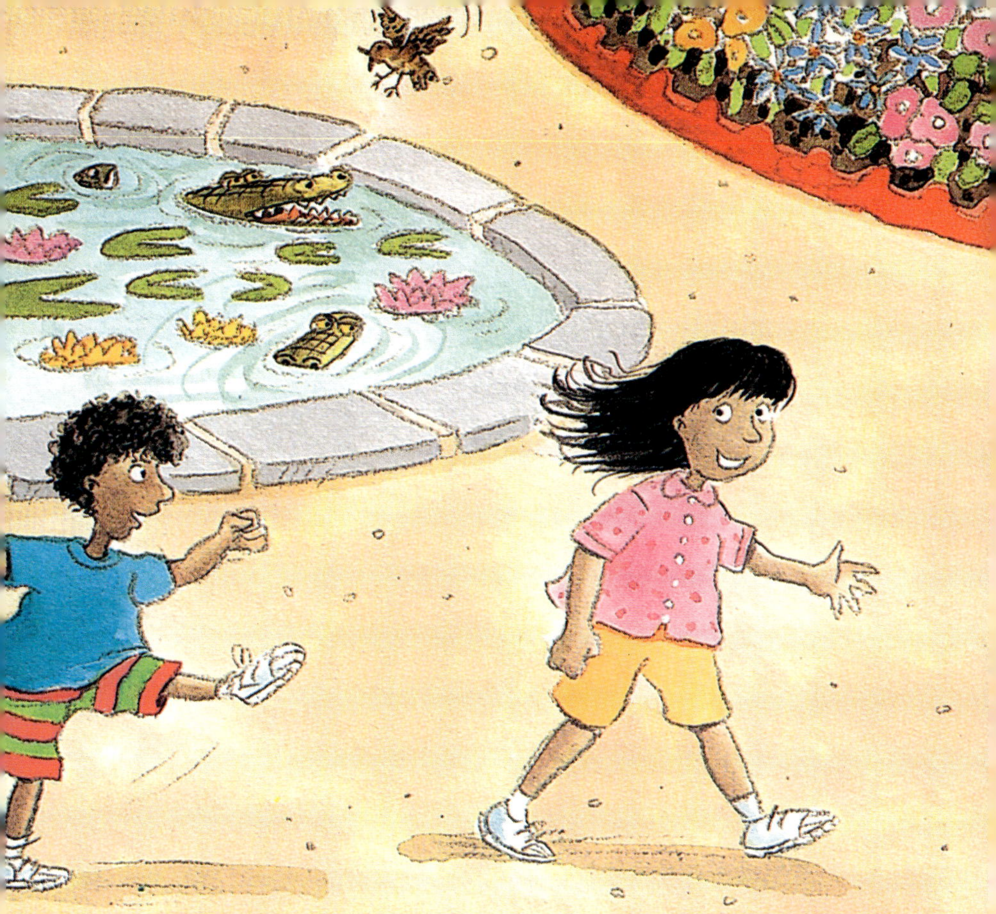

Look for crocodiles!

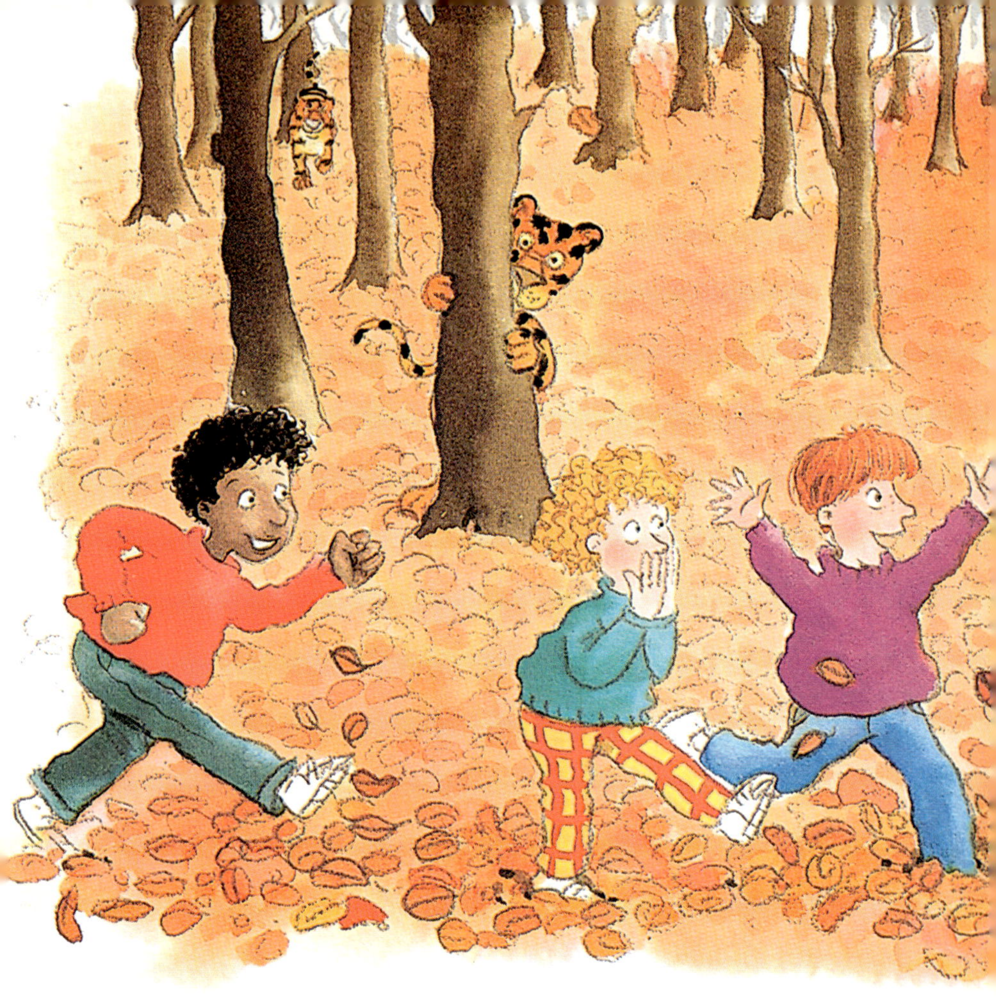

What can we do today?

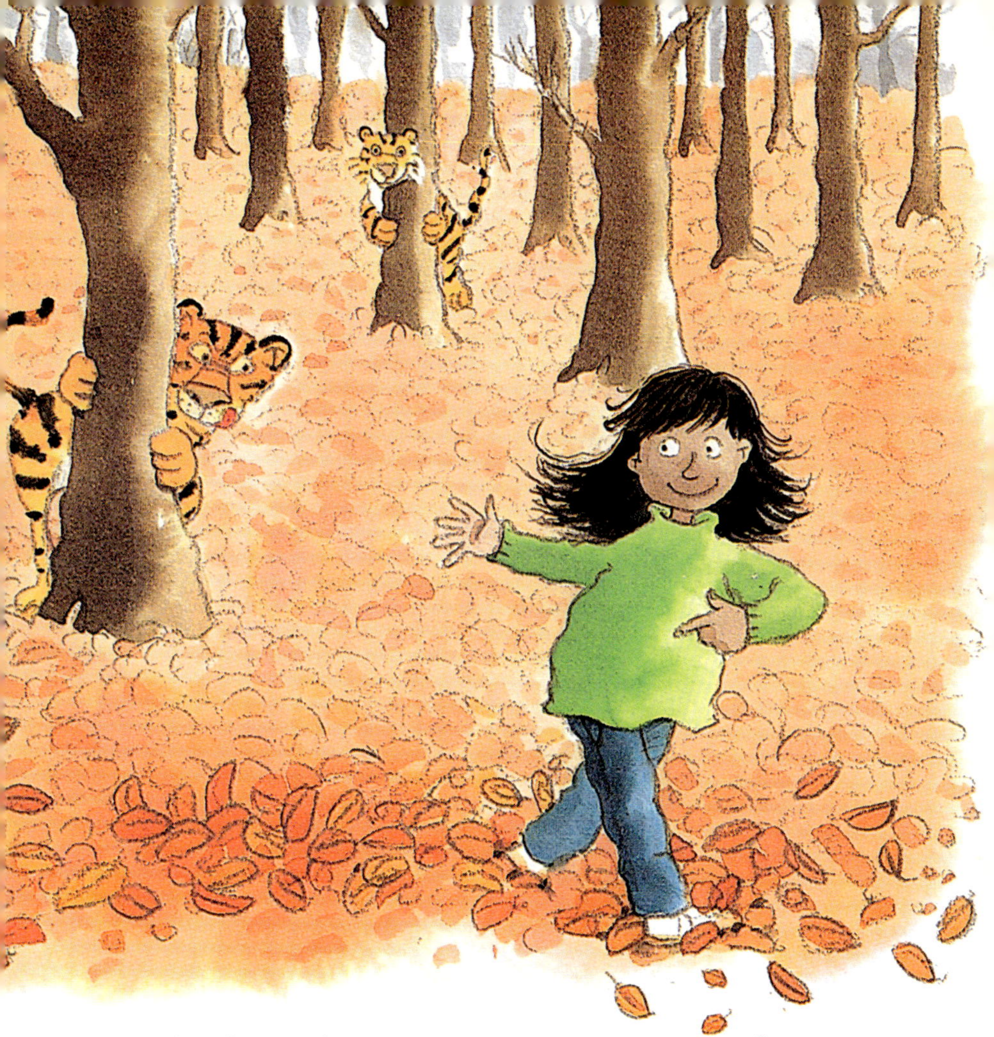

Look for tigers!

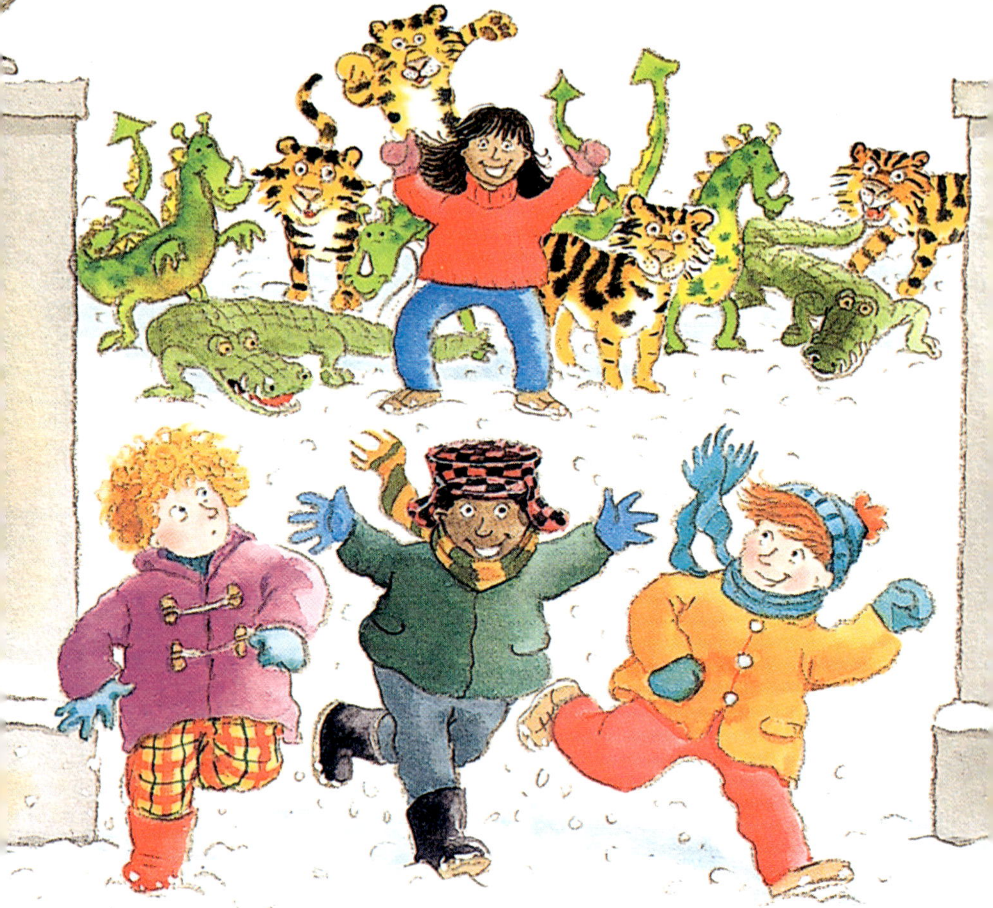

What can we do today?
Run away!